Aftermath

One Act Play
(Adult version)

Barbara Towell

TSL Drama

Foreword

Six million Jews were killed by the Nazis in World War Two. One million of these were children. In fact, Hitler was not only responsible for the death of Jews, but in addition other groups such as: gypsies, Serbs, Poles and people with learning disabilities. Overall, it is thought the Nazis exterminated seventeen million innocent people. Hitler considered them to be less than human. With aid of Darwinists and a pure breeding programme, he aimed to create a race of perfect people – an Aryan race with blond hair and blue eyes.

In his book *Mein Kampf* Hitler declared, that once he rose to power, he would eradicate Jews from Germany. Few believed he would actually do this; however, as soon as he became chancellor, he started to action his plan.

It was Hitler's intention, that eventually all Jewish people would be brought to concentration camps such as Auschwitz and Dachau. They were misled into believing that they were relocating to a better place. In these concentration camps people were virtually starving, frequently abused, forced to endure long hours of hard labour and to live in the most appalling conditions imaginable. Those who were old, sick or weak were soon killed or died of starvation. Some camps had gas chambers, where crowds were herded towards on arrival. They believed they were entering showers, only to be poisoned by gas.

My father, as a young Jewish doctor, originally from Czecho-slovakia, was part of the mission which organised and supervised the repatriation of Czech citizens from Dachau. In his memoirs he states: *What I saw later in films or pictures, could not describe adequately, the horror of what we have seen … it would be useless, impossible, to try to express this in words.*

Inspired by the poem 'Real Chocolate' by Stewart Florsheim, and my own family background, I wrote the novel, *A Little Piece for Mother*. My intention in writing this, was to show the long-term effects that prejudice, hatred and persecution have; not only on its immediate victims, but on the next generations.

From *A Little Piece for Mother* was born the youth version of the play *Aftermath*. This is included in my book of plays and performance poems: *Drama for Young Performers*. The collection not only provides opportunities to enjoy drama and develop those skills, but to be thought-provoking and informative.

Pinner Writers Group decided to stage a reading performance of the play in commemoration of Holocaust Memorial Day, 2022. It received such good feedback, that with a few changes and additions, I believed it would be a powerful, enlightening play for adult audiences. Hence this second version.

Production Notes

Although the script contains precise stage directions, I would encourage flexibility with the production. Of course, how the play is staged will very much depend on venue, numbers of actors and available finances.

In terms of costume, it is not reasonable to expect the actors, playing female characters in Auschwitz, to shave their heads. Therefore, tight head scarves binding the head should suffice in suggesting baldness. Striped garments should ideally be worn by the Jewish women as was the norm in Auschwitz.

The script states that crowds are present at the station in Auschwitz. In addition, other Jewish women and girls live in the same koje as Hania, Mamusia, Sara and Ruti. Stage directions suggest they are to be imagined. However, the director could choose to cast non-speaking roles. Although I would ask there are no major dialogue changes, it may be desirable, if the director sees fit, to add in extra short lines or utterances for these extra actors.

In order for the play not only to really touch the audience, but to give an authentic picture of what really took place in Auschwitz, I would recommend, using film footage, and even back projection showing black and white still photographs of people who died in the camp. These can be obtained free from YouTube; or at a small price from other sources. Permission may be required.

Prior to the lights going up before Scene 3, and the video footage [or sound effects] of the train arriving at Auschwitz, I would recommend playing a section of music from Henryk Mikolaj Góreckis' Symphony No. 3 Op.36. (Known as the Symphony of Sorrowful Songs.) This is a very powerful and moving piece which, in my opinion, sets the mood perfectly.

If musicians are available, it may be possible to incorporate an appropriate piece of music at the point in Scene 5 where reference is made by Hania, to Ewa being part of a group, playing welcoming music for new arrivals at Auschwitz. This will require a slight readjustment of the script. It is not indicated in the script – I offer it only as a suggestion.

I implore directors and actors to deal with the subject very sensitively, yet use imagination in getting across the truth of the Holocaust; and indeed, the evil perpetuated by prejudice.

'Aftermath'

Characters in order of appearance

Hania: Jewish, Polish girl. Age 19

Jelena: helper/staff in Rehabilitation Camp

Dusha: helper/staff in Rehabilitation Camp

Ewa: Jewish Polish girl. Hania's sister. Age 17

Mamusia: Mother of Hania and Ewa

Sara: Jewish girl. Friend of Hania's family

Ruti: Jewish girl. Friend of Hania's family

Kapo: Zosia Supervisor in Auschwitz

Guard 1:   Nazi Guard

Guard 2:   Nazi Guard

Obersturmfüher Weissner: superior SS Officer

Oberschütze Kranze: lower rank SS Officer

Narrator

Properties

Bench/item to represent this and a bed
Table for preparation of drinks and cake
Plates, mugs or cups and saucers, tea spoons, tea or coffee pot,
kettle
Tray
Cake
Bars of chocolate
Crusts/pieces of bread
Comfortable chair for Hania
Violin case
Whips and sticks used by Guards and Kapo Zosia
Pistols

GLOSSARY

Koje – hut lived in by those imprisoned in Auschwitz.
Kanada – sheds where inmates worked sorting clothes and
belongings from new arrivals at Auschwitz.

Running time:
Approximately 60/70 minutes.

House lights down

[Back projection/sound effects of concentration camp from WW2]

Scene 1

Dormitory inside Rehabilitation Camp 1945

In darkness

HANIA: *[Screams]*

Spot on HANIA *sitting up in bed screaming. Pulls back covers and looks at her feet.*

Lights up   Spot off

HANIA: Rats! Rats they bite toes, my feet! I stay not where rats! [*Jumps out of bed, still yelling at the invisible rats.*]

JELENA: [*Enter stage right. Rushes towards* HANIA. *In loud, gentle whisper.*] Hania, Hania! Sshh! Come. Come back to bed! Hush, I promise there are no rats here. Not here. Come. Quiet. Let's get you back into bed. All is well. Shh! Shh! No rats. I promise.

HANIA: [*Sits on bed. Shows her feet to* JELENA. *Points to scars.*] Look you see. See bites... do not tell me no rats! See where bites. There, and there. They come in. Every night they come... crawling through that hole [*Points downwards to the wall by her bed.*]

JELENA: They are old scars from rats in that other place. [*Gently*] Come now, quiet. Quiet. You don't want to wake... upset the others. I help you back to bed... just bad dreams. Dreams from that place. You are not in Auschwitz now. Come now, Hania.

[JELENA *settles* HANIA *back in bed and arranges covers over her.* HANIA *sits up again.*]

HANIA: But I see them. The rats, they come through that hole – from garden. [*Points again to the supposed hole in the wall.*]

Lights down

Scene 2

Next day. Afternoon.
Day room in Rehabilitation Camp.

Lights up

DUSHA *is preparing mugs/cups and saucers, drinks and cakes at side of stage.* HANIA *is sitting in a comfortable chair further away in corner, staring into space.*

DUSHA: [*Calls towards off stage right.*] Jelena... Jelena!

[JELENA *enters stage left, carrying some towels.*]

DUSHA: Oh! There you are. It is almost time for afternoon drinks. Do you think you could give me a hand?

JELENA: That will be no problem. Of course. I just put away these towels. [*Puts towels on shelf at back of stage. Walks over and helps* DUSHA.]

DUSHA: [*Looks over at* HANIA.] I worry about that one sometimes.

JELENA: Hania?

DUSHA: Yes, Hania, the Polish girl. She sits there day after day in the corner, just staring out of the window as if at nothing. Hardly ever says a word. Well, not during the day.

JELENA: She is not alone in that – most of these poor people in this rehabilitation camp, they are gaunt, solemn – like stone statues – far away as if in another world. [*Pause*] She eats, yes? Hania eats something today?

DUSHA: A little bread at breakfast. A morsel – not much. Not like some who can't seem to get enough food. Look at her. She is so very thin – exceptionally thin – although I often see her grab pieces of bread from the table – eyes darting around before squirreling it away inside her sleeve or pocket, before anyone can see – or so she thinks.

JELENA: Here, give me the knife and I slice cake. [*Cuts the cake into slices*. DUSHA *distributes slices to different plates*.] My, they have all suffered so much in ways we can only imagine. The concentration camp, that Auschwitz – such a place. Worse than hell.

Lights down

Projection of photo shots from Auschwitz.

Lights up

DUSHA: And now they are here... but still, not really here. Not really with us. Rehabilitation? Well, we try to help. [*Pause*] Liberation. Hard for some to realise. Each person, of course, is different. [*Pause*] I can't put my finger on it, but there is something about that young woman which troubles me.

JELENA: Maybe it helps that we changed her bed.

DUSHA: Oh! I did not know this.

JELENA: Yes, last night – of course, you were not on duty – we moved Hania's bed from being by the window. Luckily, Gerda, the Dutch lady, very kindly suggested they swap.

DUSHA: That is good. Let us now hope it makes the difference and she won't so often wake with such ear-piercing screams – such haunting nightmares.

JELENA: Have you seen the scars on her feet – on her toes – where the rats have left their mark? Half of one of her left toes is missing.

DUSHA: I have. Poor Hania. No wonder she has nightmares. [*Looks at her watch*.] Oh! Look at the time! We need to give out the drinks and cake. [*Pause*] I nearly forgot. [*Hurries off stage and returns, carrying a largish box.*] There's a treat for everyone today. Came in the food parcels.

JELENA: Well, what is it? [*Goes to help* DUSHA *open box.* DUSHA, *laughingly, pulls it back.*]

DUSHA: Wait and see. [*Opens box. Takes out chocolate bars.*] Chocolate!

JELENA: My goodness! That will be a real treat. But we take care not to give them too much. Chocolate is very rich, I think. We don't want to upset anyone's stomach.

DUSHA: [*Chuckles*] There is not that much chocolate here. A few squares for each person. Should be fine for everyone. Well, almost everyone. We take care anyway.

Lights down

Lights up

HANIA *sits in comfortable chair beside a small coffee table, centre stage. She is looking vacant and twists fingers.*

DUSHA: [*Enters. She carries tray with a mug and plate with a slice of cake on it. Walks towards* HANIA. *Puts tray on table.*] Hania.

HANIA: [*Jumps with fright.*] Oh!

DUSHA: I am sorry. I didn't mean to frighten you. Would you like hot drink?

HANIA: [*Irritably*] No. No, thank you.

DUSHA: Perhaps a little something to eat? You hardly ate anything at lunchtime.

HANIA: I am fine – eat plenty. I am not used to more than one feed a day.

DUSHA: [*Takes a chocolate bar from her apron pocket.*] Ah! I have something here tempting. I feel sure you will like this. [*Breaks a few squares of chocolate from* *bar and offers it to* HANIA.] Here, some chocolate for you.

HANIA: [*Angrily shouts.*] Chocolate! I do not eat chocolate. [*Stands up. Pushes back chair and exits.*]

DUSHA: Hania! Hania! [*Starts to follow her. Then stops and turns to* JALENA *as she enters.*]

JALENA: Wow! What a reaction! Shall I go to her?

DUSHA: No, I think it best to leave her for a while. Let's go and see to the others. Marenka was not too well earlier, and then there is Marta – she has been very weepy today.

JALENA: So, maybe later we find Hania. She may be calmer then.

DUSHA: Yes. Good idea. I expect she will be in the garden sitting on the usual bench by the apple tree.

Lights down

Lights up

Later same day in garden.

HANIA *dozes on bench. Enter* DUSHA. *Walks slowly to* HANIA.

DUSHA: [*Touches* HANIA's *shoulder gently.* HANIA *leaps in fright.*] I am so sorry, Hania. I didn't mean to frighten you. I just come now to see if there's anything I can get you? Anything you need? [*Pause*] It is beginning to get chilly now evening's coming and the sun's going in. Perhaps a shawl or cardigan? [HANIA *stands, is shaking and looking alarmed.*] Are you all right, Hania?

HANIA: [*Looks at* DUSHA.] All right? Is anyone here, all right? How could I possibly be all right?

DUSHA: Of course. Of course. I am sorry. [*Pause*] Look,

would it help to talk... to talk about what happened... perhaps what happened there in that place...

HANIA: Talk? No. No, I do not want to talk. [*Walks away. Stops. Turns to face* DUSHA.] Sorry. I am so sorry. I do not wish to be rude. I know you... and many others here in this... what do you call it, Rehabilitation Camp? [DUSHA *nods agreement.*] try your best to help... and I thank you for that. But I try to forget, not talk about the past. [*Pause*] In fact, I need to constantly remind myself – remember, exactly where – where it is I am now.

Lights down

[DUSHA *remains still. Spotlight on* HANIA. *She gets up and moves centre stage, facing audience.*]

HANIA: I cannot believe it! The marching is over. Death marches, that is what people here are calling them. It is amazing to realise that against all the odds I have somehow survived – am at last... free. I cannot take it in – the daily torment is over. [*Walks from one side of stage to next, as if checking no guard is looking for her. Returns to centre, looking into audience.*] Yet what does freedom really mean? No more Nazi guards? Cruel Kapos? But what of the nightmares, the evils that constantly haunt us, twist our spirits inside out? [*Pause*] I do not think it possible to be free – to be absolutely free – ever. Is there hope for me? A future? [*Pause*] Who would believe it, that on that day we arrived at Auschwitz, after that terrible, terrible train journey, we all still had hope?

Spot off

Scene 3

Auschwitz

Sound

Train pulling into station at Auschwitz. The wagons' sides being opened. People crying and shouting to get out of the train. Marching and shouting commands of SS Guards.

Lights up

SS Guards 1 & 2: [*Enter stage from different directions. Ad lib, shouting at Jews getting off the train.*] Alle Raus! Alle Raus! Alle Raus! Mach schnell! Alle Raus! Mach schnell!

[*Enter HANIA and EWA. EWA is clutching violin case. They appear traumatised as they start to walk slowly as if in a large crowd.*]

EWA: So many people. [*Turns as if crowds pushing from behind.*] Hey stop pushing. Why all the pushing? What's the rush? We are here, aren't we? Oh! I feel so dizzy. Quite sick. [*Drops violin case and stops walking.*]

HANIA: Ewa, don't stop. You'll feel better soon, now we are out of those foul wagons and in the fresh air. Come on, Keep up. Don't slow down for goodness' sake. We will get separated from Mamusia and Tatuś. [*Points to somewhere in the distance.*] I can only just see them over there. [*Looks down at EWA who is on her knees searching for her violin.*] What are you doing down there? Get up! [*Tugs at EWA's clothing.*]

EWA: My violin! My violin case! I've dropped it, Hania! [*Points to a spot somewhere ahead.*] It's under those people's legs! [*Dives ahead as if to grab violin case.*] There it is! I must get it.

HANIA:	Ewa! Leave it. Come on, hurry before those guards over there see us.
EWA:	I must have it, Hania! I have to. Oh no! I can't see it now! It's disappeared!
HANIA:	Just leave it, I say! Come on! See those SS Guards are coming over here. Do you want to get a beating too? Just look at them. They are leaving people for dead. And besides, we mustn't lose sight of Mamusia and Tatuś. [*Sees violin. Moves towards it and grabs it.*] Oh! Look. There it is. I've got it. Get up Ewa! Here. [*Thrusts it at* EWA *who takes it.*] Take your blesséd violin – and look after it this time. And may the blesséd violin bring you peace. Come on. Hurry. [*They begin to walk again.*]
EWA:	Thank you. Thank you. [*Loudly with fear.*] That guard, he is coming over here!
GUARD 1:	[*Moves towards* HANIA *and* EWA, *waving stick. Hits* HANIA *on back with stick.*] Move! Move along! Komm! Hurry up! Do you think we have all day? [*Moves off shouting – as if beating other Jews from the train.*]
HANIA:	In God's name, we are going as fast as we can! We can't go any quicker.
EWA:	These SS Guards, they beat everyone it seems! Look. And can you see the dogs over there? Alsatians! I don't like this place at all, Hania. I think we die here. [*Voice gradually gets louder.*] I do not think we live long. The rumours we heard in the ghetto before we got here were right. We will die here. I know this already, these Nazis really do hate us Jews... and are going to kill us! [*Cries loudly.*]
HANIA:	Hush, Ewa, hush – please. Just do as the guards tell you. Then all will be well.

EWA: Everyone could not wait for that train to reach its destination. Anyone who was even half alive, pushing and shoving to be first out. All of us in hope of something better than in the ghetto we left behind – and the stench of those vile wagons that brought us here. But now? Now we are here – where is that hope?

HANIA: Ewa, calm down. [*Slows down. Taps* EWA *on shoulder.*] Hey! Look. [*Points to gate with 'Arbeit macht frei' at top.*] They are not going to kill us. It's a work camp! See. Look up there – at the inscription above the gate. 'Arbeit macht frei'. [*With relief.*] It means: work makes us free. They want us to work for them. We'll be fine.

SOUND *Dogs barking in the distance.*

Lights down

Scene 4

Garden of Rehabilitation Camp. Same day as Scene 2.

Lights up

HANIA *is sitting on bench.*

SOUND *Bark of a dog in the distance*

HANIA: [*Sighs. Looks afraid.*] A dog barks. – I am back in Auschwitz, my back pressing against a wall as one of the drooling beasts, with an open cage of gnashing teeth, bounds up and bites me. I am back in the ice-cold koje, spending nights, six to a shelf in the wooden bunk bed with a background of screams, terrorising the darkness. [*Pause*] How ironic that when in Auschwitz, I dreamed of being at home in Poland with Mamusia, Tatuś and Ewa. Now? All I dream about – have nightmares about – is of being back there in Auschwitz. [*Pause*] Whose eyes do I see again and again – and again? Night after night – and even in my daydreams? His. Those pale blue penetrating eyes. His.

Lights fade. Spot on Obersturmfüher WEISSNER, *standing as a freeze frame on the other side of the stage.*

Scene 5

Inside koje.

SOUND *Wind whistling outside.*

Lights up

HANIA *and* SARA *sit on floor shivering – centre stage.*

HANIA: [*Calls to* MAMUSIA *off stage.*] Mamusiu, come, leave Ruti to sleep. [MAMUSIA *enters stage left.*] She is quiet now. Sit with Sara and me. Come, we huddle together – try to keep warm.

[MAMUSIA *huddles close to* HANIA *and* SARA.]

MAMUSIA: Poor Ruti, she is so unwell. I wish I could do something to make her better. [*Sighs. Rubs her hands together in an attempt to warm them.*] Those women who escaped from the next koje, I hope they will not be found. But at the same time, if they are not, I dread to think who they will pick to shoot instead. Please God, may you pick me and spare my children.

HANIA: Mamusiu! Don't say such things. [*Pause*] God! It's freezing in here!

SARA: It is more freezing out there – and the wind, it bites to the marrow.

HANIA: And every one of my bones tells me this, Sara. I feel as if I am already dead. I wish they had not chosen such a day to escape. Three times we already marched out and lined up for Zählappell. I despise these roll calls.

MAMUSIA: There will be a fourth, I feel sure. The women would have been found by now if they were somewhere near. They'll be miles away by this time, for sure.

HANIA: Ooh my belly, it aches – I really need to eat.

SARA: Well, there'll be no food for any of us, Hania. You know that. Our punishment for their escape.

HANIA: [*Stands up and walks about in an attempt to get warm.*] Twelve hours every damn day I work in that shed, in sub-zero temperatures – all that sorting of clothes – clothes that could be keeping us warm! And all that, makes me ravenous. [*Sits down with the other two again.*] My legs, they feel like jelly, standing all day, then at the end of it, endless roll calls – being counted again and again – as if those idiot, sadistic guards had made a mistake the first time.

RUTI: [*Enter stage left, groaning in pain and clutching her stomach.*] I need to go to the latrines. Now!

MAMUSIA: [*Gets up and goes to comfort* RUTI.] I would take you myself if I could. You know that...

SARA: [*To* MAMUSIA.] But you know you can't. It's not our time yet. You'll just have to hold on, Ruti.

RUTI: [*Crying*] Please, I cannot wait... I cannot... I must go to latrines.

HANIA: Ruti, you know the rules – you have heard the Sheisskapo yourself. You will have to do your best to wait. I wish... we all wish things were different.

MAMUSIA: [*Feeling* RUTI's *forehead.*] She feels so hot. I take you back to bunk, Ruti. Come. [*Helps* RUTI *to walk to bunk bed. They exit stage left.*]

HANIA: I don't think she will be able to march out for another Zählappell, do you? She can barely walk, let alone stand in a roll call.

SARA: Well, she'll have to somehow. It's out, or be shot. Did you not see the Rapportführer? His face was like thunder, spitting venom and threats of insufferable punishments. [*Jumps up.*] Oh God! I can't stand it in here. It stinks. I'm going out for some air! [*Exit stage right.*]

MAMUSIA: [*Enter stage left. Sits beside* HANIA.] So cruel not to let us use latrines when we need to. Leaving us with no human dignity.

HANIA: That's exactly what the pigs want. [*Pause*] Poor Ruti. She doesn't deserve this.

MAMUSIA: She tries now to sleep. I tell her, she will feel better when she wakes... but I know this not to be the truth. [*Sighs*] I wonder how is Ewa?

HANIA: Yesterday, I saw her playing in the orchestra, welcoming newcomers to this 'wonderful' place as they get off the train. [*Pause*] I don't know why they even bother to do that. It isn't long before they'll be learning the truth — those who survive being gassed, that is.

MAMUSIA: The music, it makes them calmer, more manageable.

HANIA: Yes, tricks everyone into a sense of false security.

MAMUSIA: [*Sighs*] All those violin lessons — who would have thought Ewa would end up playing it for Nazis, in a camp like this?

HANIA: And so lucky it wasn't lost! Bet they don't keep their precious orchestra hungry. [*Pause. Clutches stomach.*] Mind you, I wouldn't relish entertaining those fat Nazi pigs as they stuff their faces every evening at dinner, sing their bawdy songs and drink themselves under the table. All that food... when we are literally starving. My belly aches it's so empty. [*Gets up and walks around the stage. Gestures to all the Jews in the Koje. Loudly.*] Look at us all — freezing, starving, longing to get out of this hell hole...

MAMUSIA: [*In loud whisper. Kneeling up and taking a small piece of bread from inside top garment.*] Shhh! Stop shouting. Come here and sit. [HANIA *sits down beside* MAMUSIA *who offers her the piece of bread.*] Take, Child. I save from yesterday. It is very hard, I know, but better than nothing.

HANIA: Thank you, but I am not a child, Mamusiu. I am nineteen, almost twenty – I'll be fine. Yesterday, you persuaded me to share your soup, I cannot take this too. If you do not eat, you become sick – you cannot work – then what happens? Like all those others, you disappear – disappear and I will never see you again. We have lost Tatuś. We rarely see Ewa. I do not want to lose you too.

MAMUSIA: And you? You had nothing, but a little watery soup for more than a day. A mother she cannot watch her child starve.

HANIA: [*Gets up and starts to walk around, accusingly glaring at the other occupants of the koje.*] And I have not forgotten why I had nothing. The moment my back was turned, seeing to Ruti, my food bowl disappeared. Some thieving shite... stole it! [*Loudly*] Yes, one of you lot in this very koje! [*Walks to front of stage. Looks into audience. Points randomly at different people.*] Was it you? Was it you? Or you? We should be looking after each other, we Jews – but no – it's dog eat dog in this hell hole. [*Walks from one side of the stage to the other, looking accusingly into audience. Turns and walks towards others elsewhere on stage. Then returns to centre stage. Stands still. Looks out into audience.*] But if I get my hands on whoever left me with an empty belly, they will be lucky to survive to tell the tale. [*Shouts*] You hear that, all of you!

MAMUSIA:	[*Gets up. Hurries to* HANIA.] No! No! Do not say such things. [*Offers bread.*] Now take. And eat.
HANIA:	I will not! [*Exits stage right.*]

Lights down

[*Spot on* SARA *standing outside the Koje.* HANIA *enters and stands next to her, frowning.*]

SARA:	Oh, it's you. What's wrong?
HANIA:	What's right?
SARA:	True. Look at those guards over there. They're going frantic – half-crazed, searching for those women. No chance. Gone too long. And good luck to them, I say. [*Pause*] You know, it's almost funny, watching them yelling and blaming each other. But to be fair, I think some of the younger SS Guards are like us, living in fear of their great and wonderful leaders. [*Pause. Looks across to other side of stage. Lowers voice*]. Don't look now, but over there is a new SS Officer. He's been lurking outside our koje since I came out. [*Spot on* WEISSNER *standing in another part of stage or auditorium.*]
HANIA:	As if we didn't have enough Nazi pigs here already.
SARA:	Keep your voice down Hania, for goodness' sake.
HANIA:	He can't hear, he's too far off.
SARA:	You never know. [*Pulls* HANIA *over to another part of stage. Spot follows.*] Actually, he doesn't look quite so hard-nosed as most of the officers.
HANIA:	He'd shoot just the same though. Believe me, looks are deceptive.
SARA:	Some girl who was passing a minute or two ago, told me he's called Obersturmfüher Weissner. Come straight from the Russian Front. Said she saw him snooping round Kanada. Maybe you've

even already seen him since you work there? You can't see it clearly now, but he has brown hair – sort of escaping from under his cap – and these very piercing blue eyes.

HANIA: Perhaps, but I wouldn't know because I don't look at the pigs – unless I absolutely have to that is.

SARA: Come, let us go inside, the wind's getting up and I am freezing.

Spot off

Lights up

Inside Koje.

HANIA *and* SARA *enter stage right. Followed by* MAMUSIA *who enters stage left.*

SARA: How is Ruti now?

MAMUSIA: [*Sighs*] Not so good. Not good at all, Sara. Come, let us all pray. [*Kneels and beckons to* SARA, HANIA *and others in koje to join her.* SARA *kneels.* HANIA *remains standing.*]

HANIA: And a lot of good that has done us all so far.

MAMUSIA: [*Firmly*] Hania, please. [HANIA *remains standing, but closes eyes respectfully while others pray.*] May His illustrious name become great and holy in the world that he created. May abundant peace from heaven, and His life be upon us – and especially upon our dear Ruti. May He who makes peace in His high places, make peace here... here in this, this... place. And let us say Amen.

KAPO ZOSIA: [*Off stage.*] Out! Come on – out you lot. Hurry! Get into line!

SARA: [*Jumps up.*] Oh no! It's Kapo Zosia! She's worse than the Nazi pigs that one.

KAPO ZOSIA: [*Enter stage right.*] I said, another count. What are you lot doing in here still? Out all of you! Move! [*Threatening with whip.*] Out at once. I tell you no more times!

[ALL *get up. Walk reluctantly to stage right.*]

KAPO ZOSIA: [*Looks to off stage left.*] Who's that over in that bunk, refusing to move?

[KAPO ZOSIA *walks quickly towards stage left.*

MAMUSIA *turns. Hurries to* KAPO ZOSIA.]

KAPO ZOSIA: Get up, you!

MAMUSIA: It's Ruti. She's sick. Really sick.

KAPO ZOSIA: [*Pulls* RUTI *in from off stage. She is delirious and can barely stand up.*] Come on you! Out with the others.

HANIA: [*Rushes back and helps* MAMUSIA *hold* RUTI *up as she begins to fall down.*] For mercy sake! Can't you see she can barely walk, let alone stand for hours in yet another roll call in the freezing cold?

KAPO ZOSIA: [*To* Ruti.] What is it? You prefer to lie in your own crap, do you?

SARA: [*Walks towards* RUTI.] She was desperate, and still the Scheisskapo refused to let her go to the latrines!

KAPO ZOSIA: Watch your tongue, girl. Latrine times – in morning and evening – when told! You know the rules.

SARA: Our noses certainly do.

KAPO ZOSIA: [*Lashes* SARA *with whip. She then turns to look at* RUTI *who is hardly able to stay upright even when held by* HANIA *and* MAMUSIA. *She moans quietly.*] Right. Leave her where she is. If she refuses to get out, the guards will deal with that! The rest of you – do you hear me – OUT! Now! [*Lashes whip. Pushes* HANIA.]

Lights down

Lights up – dim

> [RUTI *lies in centre of stage, softly moaning.* GUARDS 1 & 2 *enter. A second or two later* HANIA *enters running towards* RUTI. *Stops when sees* GUARDS *and pulls back, not wanting to be seen by them as they have their backs to her, looking down at* RUTI. HANIA *retreats. She cautiously watches in koje doorway at side of stage.*]

GUARD 1: What is this? [*Pushes at* RUTI *with his* foot.] Is it dead?

GUARD 2: No, it is moaning.

GUARD 1: And it stinks. Get up bit of filth! [*Kicks* RUTI.] I said up, Judenschwein. Alle Raus! Now! Alle raus!

GUARD 2: It refuses to obey.

GUARD 1: Nothing else for it then. [HANIA *exits as* GUARD 1 *takes out pistol.*]

Lights down.

SOUND *Gunshot in darkness.*

Scene 6

Next evening. Inside koje.

Lights up

HANIA, MAMUSIA *and* SARA *are sitting centre stage inside the koje.* HANIA *gets up. Walks towards stage right.* MAMUSIA *gets up and follows her.*

MAMUSIA: Hania, where are you going?

HANIA: Out of this hole. I'm starving. Need to eat in peace.

MAMUSIA: But make sure you are back in time for Zählappell.

HANIA: I am not a child anymore, Mamusiu.

MAMUSIA: A mother she always worries however old her children. [*Walks away and sits down.*]

SARA: [*Gets up and walks to* HANIA *who stops and turns to face* SARA.] But you do need to be careful, Hania. That Obersturmfüher Weissner is about. I heard today that although he may not look as much like an Arayan Nazi pig, he is in fact no different. Just as loathsome.

HANIA: I go just behind the koje. [*Points all around koje and at audience.*] I cannot stand these women staring – begging. [*Points into audience.*] That one over in the corner – see? New a few days ago. She snatched bread from Mamusia's hand yesterday. And Mamusia, she did nothing. Let her take it. But not me.

SARA: That one. She's hardly more than a child and not used to being starved.

HANIA: Huh! She soon will be. [*Nods towards audience as if to girl.*] Even now she stares at me. I can't stand the sight of her. I go.

SARA: Also watch out for that fat ruddy faced guard too. No doubt he's prowling around as usual. They are all very edgy tonight.

HANIA: Him. I know the one you mean – looks remarkably like Hitler with that toothbrush moustache. [*Exits*]

Lights down

Lights up

Scene 7

Same day. A few moments later outside the koje.

HANIA *is standing at the side of stage, as if leaning against the wall of the koje.*

HANIA: Peace at last. [*Takes out piece of bread from inside her top.*] And if there is a God, I thank you that I have managed to hold on to this piece of bread. Certainly, wasn't going to let anyone steal my food again. [*Starts to gnaw hard bread.*] How we manage to survive, eating such stale bread is a wonder. [*Picks at bread.*] Come out you pesky insect [*Looks at it between her fingers.*] Maybe I shall just eat you. After all, Mamusia tells me not to waste the protein. [*Eats insect.*]

[WEISSNER *and* KRANZE *enter stage left. Stop when spot* HANIA.]

WEISSNER: [*To* HANIA.] Du!

[HANIA *ignores* WEISSNER. *Quickly finishes eating the bread.*]

WEISSNER: [*Loudly*] Judenschwein, did you hear me?

HANIA: [*Quietly and insolently, without looking at* WEISSNER] What?

WEISSNER: [*Shouts*] Komm her!

[KRANZE *lashes whip threateningly.*]

KRANZE: Ah! Now she comes.

WEISSNER: If she was not a filthy lice-ridden Jewish whore, Oberschütze Kranze, she would be quite attractive.

KRANZE: [*Sneering*] But without hair, she is nothing but a shaven Jewish pig.

WEISSNER: True. Look at her. She is scared.

KRANZE: [*Chuckles*] You are right – as of course, you always are Obersturmfüher.

[*They walk around* HANIA *as if examining an object.*]

WEISSNER: You think she is too thin? Could it be possible for her to be a little hungry?

KRANZE: But she has been eating – we saw her eat. A good supper was it not, Judenschwein?

HANIA: What do you think?

KRANZE: Obersturmfüher, you know what I think? We have a very insolent Judenschwein here.

WEISSNER: [*Calmly*] Lively. Spirited, this one. [*Much louder.*] Aren't you? [*Pause. Calm, flat expression.*] She makes no reply. Perhaps she is still hungry? [*Pause*] Are you hungry, Judenschwein?

[KRANZE *lashes whip.*]

WEISSNER: No. Stop Obershütze. No need for that. Not at the moment. Let me see. Let me see what I have here in my jacket pocket. [*Takes out some chocolate. Pause. With mock surprise, looks at* HANIA *who looks at it.*] Oh! You show interest now. [*Moves closer to* HANIA, *holding out chocolate.*]

HANIA: [*With guarded enthusiasm.*] What's that? Chocolate?

WEISSNER: It speaks. What is that it said, Kranze?

HANIA: [*With increased enthusiasm.*] I said chocolate. Is it chocolate?

WEISSNER: You come closer if you want to see.

[HANIA *moves closer.* WEISSNER *holds the chocolate close to* HANIA.]

WEISSNER: You like chocolate? I see it in your eyes, you love chocolate.

KRANZE: Yah! Yah! It is true.

WEISSNER: [*Gently*] Komm here. Komm here. [HANIA *hesitates.*] Closer. [HANIA *steps closer.* WEISSNER *holds chocolate close to her nose.*] Yes, Komm, smell it. I am certain a girl, a Jewish girl like you, has not eaten chocolate for a very long time. Am I right? [*Pause*] How many years?

HANIA: [*Politely*] I don't know. I'm not sure. [*Her hand rises to take the chocolate, but stops.*]

WEISSNER: [*In kindly tone*] Here, take it.

[HANIA *quickly reaches out her hand to grab the chocolate.* WEISSNER *pulls it back.*]

WEISSNER: [*Angrily*] No. No, you grab. Snatching and grabbing is very bad manners, Is it not? [*Pause as* WEISSNER *waits for* HANIA *to reply.*]

KRANZE: [*Shouts*] Speak when Obersturmfüher Weissner asks you a question!

[*Kicks* HANIA.]

HANIA: Ouch! What was that for?

KRANZE: If you refuse to speak when spoken to, there will be another kick and that will really hurt. Or maybe something worse. [*Pause*] See how generous and kind the Obersturmfüher is. Show respect, Judenschwein.

WEISSNER: [*Taunting*] So – do you think you deserve chocolate? Good German chocolate?

[HANIA *does not reply.*] Well? [*Still* HANIA *does not reply.*]

KRANZE: [*Takes out pistol. Points it at* HANIA.] This might help.

WEISSNER: Well?

HANIA: [*Whispers*] No.

WEISSNER: I cannot hear you, Jewish whore.

HANIA: No.

WEISSNER: [*With sweet sarcasm.*] No, of course not! [*Spits at HANIA.*]

HANIA: [*Covers face with hands.*] Urgh! Oh my God!

WEISSNER: [*Holds out chocolate in direction of KRANZE.*] Here take these pieces [*pointing to Alsatian in the distance.*] and give to the dog over there. He does deserve chocolate.

KRANZE: [*Takes the chocolate.*] Yah! Obersturmfüher Weissner. At once. [*He marches off. Exit stage left.*]

WEISSNER: [*Walks away without looking at HANIA. Exits stage right.*]

SARA: [*Enter stage left. Hurries towards HANIA who is frantically wiping off the saliva from her face.*] I saw from back there. I saw him... spit at you. The disgusting, filthy Nazi swine! Oh Hania! Hania! Why did he do that?

HANIA: You did not see? [*Walks away from SARA.*]

SARA: [*Follows HANIA.*] See what? I only just came out from the Koje.

HANIA: Reason? ... They don't need a reason.

Lights down

Lights up

Scene 8

Rehabilitation camp. Garden.

HANIA: [*Sitting on bench.*] Chocolate. Now I cannot even think about chocolate without feeling sick to my stomach. [*Stands. Walks to front, centre stage. Faces audience.*] Not once, but often, Weissner tempted me – taunted me with it... and sometimes I just could not...

Lights down

Lights up – dim

[HANIA *enters from side of stage. Walks quickly. Seconds later enter* WEISSNER *and* KRANZE *from the opposite side.* HANIA *stops when sees them. Turns to walk back the way she came.*]

WEISSNER: Ah! Look who it is. The Jewish whore. The one who loves chocolate. Stop, Jewish whore!

[HANIA *stops. Momentarily she glances at them, then looks away.*]

KRANZE: I do not think it can be very hungry today, Obersturmfüher. Perhaps it has had a good meal already?

WEISSNER: And does not want chocolate? [*Takes chocolate from pocket and unwraps part of the bar.*] This gut German chocolate?

[HANIA *turns and stares at the chocolate.* WEISSNER *holds it out.* HANIA *moves slowly towards it.* WEISSNER *moves it closer to her.* KRANZE *chuckles.*]

WEISSNER: [*To* KRANZE.] I think it is hungry after all. See [*To* HANIA.] Yes, Komm closer. [*Pause*] Closer.

KRANZE: Yah! Yah! Take it, Judenschwein.

[HANIA *moves forward to take the chocolate.* WEISSNER *throws it to the ground before she has a chance to take it from him.* HANIA *crouches down. Hurriedly, looks for the chocolate.* WEISSNER *and* KRANZE *laugh as* HANIA *gobbles up pieces as well as mud from the ground.*]

KRANZE: Ha! Ha! Look, it eats the mud. Chocolate and mud the same to it.

[*When she finishes the chocolate,* HANIA *remains crouched, searching for pieces she might have missed.*]

SOUND *Alsatians barking.*

WEISSNER: [*To* KRANZE.] Go see what that disturbance is — why dogs bark. [*Pause*]

[*Exit* KRANZE.]

WEISSNER: [*To* HANIA.] There is even more. [WEISSNER *throws down, close to him, a small piece of chocolate.* HANIA *scrambles towards it. As she puts her hand on it,* WEISSNER *stamps on her hand with his jackboot.*]

HANIA: [*Screams*] Ouch!

WEISSNER: [*Removes foot from* HANIA's *hand. Crushes chocolate as* HANIA *rubs her hand.*] Now get up.

[HANIA *gets up. Starts to walk away.*]

WEISSNER: Komm here!

[HANIA *continues to walk.*]

WEISSNER: I said, stay, Jewish whore. Komm. See there is more chocolate. [*Takes out and shows her the chocolate.*

HANIA *stops. She moves towards* WEISSNER.]

WEISSNER: Now you move. [*Pulls back chocolate.*] But not yet. [*Points to wall at centre back stage.*] That way.

[HANIA *hesitates*.] That way – for chocolate. [*He pushes her in the direction of the wall. They stop when reach wall.* HANIA *reaches for chocolate.* WEISSNER *puts it into his pocket.*]

Turn. Face wall. Chocolate afterwards.

HANIA: No! No! Please. No!

WEISSNER: [*Turns her firmly.*] Keep your silence! And you behave – if you behave – chocolate – after.

Lights down

SILENCE

Lights up – very dim

[*Freeze frame: With back to audience,* HANIA *faces wall. Her body against it with hands above her head, flat against wall.* WEISSNER *faces the wall, his body precisely behind hers and hands on top of hers to suggest rape.*]

Lights up

[*Enter* SARA. *Looks at* WEISSNER *and* HANIA *still in the freeze frame. Exits quickly.*]

MAMUSIA: [*Enters. Screams. Runs to* WEISSNER. *Beats him on back and tries to pull him away from* HANIA. *Freeze frame ends.*] Get off! Get off – my Hania! This cannot happen! I tell you, leave the child – leave my child alone! Let her be! Please! Let her be!

HANIA: [*Turns head.*] Mamusiu! Mamusiu! [*Starts to cry.*]

MAMUSIA: Please! Leave her! She is but a girl – a girl – innocent child!

WEISSNER: [*With back to audience, adjusts trousers. Turns to* MAMUSIA. *Pushes her from him. Walks away. To* MAMUSIA] Make no mistake. Jewish girls, like your daughter, they do anything – anything for chocolate.

HANIA: No! No, Mamusiu. That is not true!

WEISSNER: [*Takes chocolate from pocket. Holds it up. To HANIA.*] Is it not true? How many times have you grovelled squirmed, begged – done anything for a piece? Hey?

MAMUSIA: No! Tell me, Child – tell me this is not true. He lie. This Nazi lie, Yes?

KRANZE: [*Enters*] Obersturmfüher, the disturbance has been – settled, and the ones... [*Stops. Looks at MAMUSIA.*]

MAMUSIA: [*Shouts at WEISSNER.*] You are monster – Nazi monster – pig! – pig! May He, the Almighty strike you down... cast you to depth of hell! [*Ad lib further verbal abuse.*]

[KRANZE *takes out pistol and points it at her.*]

[MAMUSIA *sees pistol. Stops yelling and moves further away from WEISSNER.*]

WEISSNER: [*Moves towards MAMUSIA. Stops when close. Smiles. Offers her chocolate.*] A little piece for mother?

[HANIA *darts towards WEISSNER. Spits at him.*]

WEISSNER: [*Wipes her saliva from his face. To KRANZE, while looking at HANIA.*] Shoot! Shoot the old Jewish whore.

[KRANZE *draws pistol. Shoots MAMUSIA. She falls to the ground, dead.*]

HANIA: [*Screams. Runs to MAMUSIA and kneels beside her.*] No! No! Mamusiu! Please, please don't die. [*Shakes MAMUSIA.*] Don't leave me! Mamusiu! I'm sorry. Mamusiu, so sorry. Forgive me. Please, please, Mamusiu, forgive me. I beg you. [*Sobs*]

KRANZE: [*Walks to MAMUSIA. Pushes her body with his*

foot.] Well and truly dead,

Obersturmfüher.

WEISSNER: [*Throws the chocolate at* HANIA.] Your reward. [*Turns to* KRANZE.] Komm, Obershütze Kranze. [*They walk away. Exit.*]

Lights down

Scene 9

Lights up

Rehabilitation Camp. Garden.

HANIA, *centre stage. Faces audience.*

HANIA: Nightmares. Such terrible dreams. They haunt me night and day. [*Pause*]
But perhaps now my bed is not by outside wall, I will sleep better – fewer nightmares – and then I be nicer – nicer to these kind people here – who who try their best to help us. And maybe – just maybe – in time, I will be able to erase all those memories of Auschwitz. [*Pause*] But – but how is this possible?

[*Lights dim*

HANIA *stands centre stage. She is covering her ears with her hands and looks down.*

Each character enters quickly one after the other from different parts of stage/or auditorium. They speak the lines below, loudly. Once all lines have been delivered, they are repeated again and again at the same time, getting louder to create a cacophony of sound. Characters whilst speaking, walk round the stage/ auditorium in various directions.]

GUARD 1: [*Lashing whip.*] Alle Raus! Alle Raus!

GUARD 2: [*Lashing whip.*] Mach schnell! Mach schnell!

JELENA: Rats! Rats!

EWA: My violin case! My violin case!

SARA: No food for any of us today.

MAMUSIA: A mother, she cannot watch her child starve.

RUTI: I need to go to the latrines. Now!

KAPO ZOSIA: I said, another count. Out at once! [*Lashes whip.*]

DUSHA: Some chocolate for you?

WEISSNER: Do you think you deserve chocolate?

KRANZE: Speak when Obersturmfüher asks you a question!

[*After a few minutes* WEISSNER *moves to* HANIA.]

WEISSNER: [*Loudly, to* HANIA *who still covers ears with hands, looking down.*] Do you think you deserve chocolate – gut German chocolate?

[*Once* WEISSNER *has spoken the above line, everyone instantly stops speaking and freezes. After a short pause* GUARDS 1 & 2 *march to the front of the stage. They face the audience. Stare into space.*]

GUARD 1:   It stinks. Get up, bit of filth!

GUARD 2:   It refuses to obey.

GUARD 1:   Nothing else for it then.

[*Lights down*

SOUND Pistol shots.

Spot on NARRATOR *standing side stage.*

NARRATOR: 'Forgive, but never forget. For those in the darkness are blinded from truth, and will repeat the evils of past generations.'

Spot off   *House lights up.*

About the Author

Barbara Towell lives with her husband, John, in West London. In addition to being a playwright and poet, she is the author of the successful international novel – *A Little Piece for Mother* which was the inspiration for *Aftermath*. Indeed, she has published other works in many genres.

With her husband John, she wrote the musical *Faith is the Key*, which was staged in Harrow and for the Dumfries Festival, Scotland. Her other published plays and monologues include: *Drama for Young Performers*, *Wedding Bells*, *Kenneth* – and *Night Duty*, co-written with David Stroud and staged at East Lane Theatre, Wembley, in July 2023.

She is an experienced English and Drama teacher who has enjoyed writing and directing productions over many years.

In 2013 she was lucky enough to win the Harrow Libraries' Crime Writing Competition, and prior to that, the Harrow Millennium Carol Writing Competition.

In addition to having a busy music and writing life, Barbara co-runs the Pinner Writers Group with Nick Horgan. Her aim is to inspire and help others to achieve their writing ambitions.

www.ingramcontent.com/pod-product-compliance
Lightning Source LLC
Chambersburg PA
CBHW030152200626
46812CB00016B/1815